Hamed Ali Al Rashdi graduated from the University of Arizona with a BSc degree in electrical engineering in 1988 and completed a master's degree in electrical engineering from Sultan Qaboos University in Oman in 2001. He is married with four children. He has a deep interest in reading, writing, and outdoor excursions. He is very fond of cultural diversities and is an excellent public speaker. He loves reading novels and immersing in poetry.

To the soul of my mother, to my children, and my family,
I dedicate this book.

Hamed Ali Al Rashdi

SHEIKH AL JIN

AUSTIN MACAULEY PUBLISHERS

LONDON • CAMBRIDGE • NEW YORK • SHARJAH

Ordering Information
Quantity sales: Special discounts are available on quantity purchases by corporations, associations, and others. For details, contact the publisher at the address below.

Publisher's Cataloging-in-Publication data
Rashdi, Hamed Ali Al
Sheikh Al Jin

ISBN 9798891558625 (Paperback)
ISBN 9798891558632 (ePub e-book)

Library of Congress Control Number: 2024918672

www.austinmacauley.com/us

First Published 2024
Austin Macauley Publishers LLC
40 Wall Street, 33rd Floor, Suite 3302
New York, NY 10005
USA

mail-usa@austinmacauley.com
+1 (646) 5125767

I would express my deepest gratitude to my wife for enduring the long hours I spent writing this book, to the publisher, and the editors who made this book a reality.

Preface

This is not a thousand and one nights of Arabian tales, but a semi-true story of a man who lived his life divided between two different worlds. He lived as a human in his world, with all the human life struggle, glory, and happiness. Yet he could not overcome his desire to experience another more bizarre and unfamiliar world, the Jin world. Some of the tales in this book are real, and some are the imagination of the author based on the fact told to him of the other world. We live in this life, wondering: are we alone? Yet the answer is not always clear. Some will argue in favor, and some will think that merely thinking of the idea is ridiculous. No one is forced to believe any different than what he/she originally believes in, but why not? Why can't there be another world? Why can't there be other creatures in another world? And why do we feel that we are alone? The fact that we can't see everything does not null their existence, and we can't be certain that this world is not shared with others. Anyway, when you look at it from a psychological point of view or sociological point of view, there are people who strongly believe that we are not alone in this world. This story will take you on an adventure of a lifetime, between the human world with all its bad and good, and the other world with its entire characteristics. The events described here are mixed together by the author to add a bit of thrill to the story. It does not matter if you agree or not with the author, but just sit back, relax, and enjoy a trip that you otherwise might not be able to take physically in a human world. The events in this story happened somewhere in a land that still hides plenty of mysteries, and it happened in time just before the evolution of the new technology. Transportation relied on animals, electricity was likely seen as something from the world of Jin, and communication was considered magical. Yes, the old days, that had their own share of tales and history.

Chapter One

When Saif opened his eyes, everything around him seemed different. The place he was in was transformed into a new world, and all things seemed to be in different shapes and colors. The last thing he could remember was that he was reading a chapter of the *"Book"*. He was deeply engrossed in reading when he felt a strong force lift him up and he lost consciousness. There are no mountains where he is from. The deserted placed that he was in now, however, was a green heaven. This place was certainly not familiar to him, and he had never seen it before. This place must be the destination he was seeking: it was the Jin world.

Saif was born an orphan; his father passed away while his mother was in her sixth month of pregnancy. He was raised by his grandfather, and his mother tried to compensate for the loss of his father by giving him all the attention that he needed. But Saif was different from all boys; he grew up fond of everything that was unusual. He used to spend hours playing alone or help his grandfather in the field. As a baby, he never liked to play with toys, and his great passion was to hear his grandfather's tales about the other world, the Jin world. Besides being a farmer, his grandfather was the astrologer of the town. People would come to him when seeking a new name for their new born babies; they would come to him to determine the best day to get married, or to trace a lost item. The grand book that his grandfather had was inherited from his ancestors and it had been in the family for generations. The book was his aid to most of his astrology work, and he proudly called it the *"Book"*. Grandpa would recite some words before opening the book and after finishing. Saif used to attend all the sessions and attempted to imitate his grandfather by moving his lips whenever his grandfather recited something. When Saif asked his grandfather about the language he was speaking – which was not familiar to him – the grandfather told him, 'This is the magic or the Jin language, and you are too young to understand it'.

To Saif, magic was the secret that should not be shared with everybody. And his passion for magic grew day by day. When he was three years old, he attempted to play with the charcoal after seeing how his grandfather handled it with grace, as if it weren't lit. Saif got his fingertip burned. He cried all day, and he learned never to play with fire again. Grandfather recognized that his nephew had a great passion for magic more than the field work, and he started teaching him how to read and write in the early stages of his life. He taught him the different names of the stars, their location in the sky, and how to distinguish them in the dark nights. He taught him the way to determine the horoscope by signing a number for each letter of the name, then adding and subtracting a constant factor that will give the correct horoscope for that name. For instance, if the boy's name is Ali and the mother's name is Fatima, he stressed that it was important to know the mother's name, then five points for the "A" and two for "L" and so on. The number he will get will be corresponding to a certain star in the astrological circle that he was using. The boy would practice his knowledge on other boys, and sometimes that knowledge got him into trouble. One day, he was trying to identify the horoscope of a neighbor boy, Khalfan, since he knew his name and his mother's name. It was easy for him to determine the boy's star, which turned out to be the Scorpion. Well, Khalfan didn't like the horoscope and started beating Saif, until the grandfather showed up and saved Saif from the neighbor boy's hand. He told his grandfather the story, and his grandfather cautioned him that he should be careful next time and not express his knowledge unless asked.

Not only astrology attracted Saif, even the way his grandfather was able to find lost items or stolen items amused him. His grandfather used to read the traces of the thieves and could pinpoint the exact location of a lost item. How did he do it?

"It is all in the book, my son," he used to tell his grandson. "It is just a matter of knowing where to find it."

Saif was not allowed to touch the book since he was still young and his grandfather thought that some of the knowledge might harm him. "There will be a time when you are old enough to understand the secrets of this book, but for now, you must concentrate on how to read and write nicely," his grandpa used to tell him. Saif loved his grandfather and always listened carefully to what he had to say. His mother was not very comfortable as she thought that Saif might learn some of the trade secrets of his grandfather, and she used to tell Saif not to think too much about what his grandfather did. To Saif, the Jin world was a fantasy land where all the impossible was possible. He would imagine that he could fly without wings, he could see as far as he wanted, and he could get whatever he fancied; all things that were out of reach in the human world was obtainable in the Jin world.

Saif heard his mother and his grandfather once whispering, and he stopped to eavesdrop what they were whispering about. "Now that Saif is five years old, it is time that the boy has his thing removed. I have called Humaid, the barber, to come to our house tomorrow, and he will perform the ritual," Saif's grandfather told his daughter.

"But father, the weather is hot these days, and the wound will be exposed, since the boy is always playing outside," Saif's mother said.

"Don't worry, I will explain everything to him," Grandfather said. Saif did not understand a word of what his mother and her father were whispering about, but he was certain it was something to do with him.

The next day, as usual, Saif rushed outside to play. He used a palm tree leaf stem and put it between his legs and pretended that he was riding a horse. In his right hand, he would carry a stick and wave it like a sword. Running up and down the pathway in front of his house, he suddenly heard three gunshots coming from his house direction. Saif froze in his place. He did not know what to do or why there was a gun fire coming from his house. Then he rushed back into the house to see what was going on. He met his grandfather at the door, who escorted him to the room upstairs. There sat Humaid with a barber knife in one hand, a cotton bud on the other, and a big tin pot in front of him.

"Oh, there you are! Come, boy, don't be afraid," Humaid addressed Saif with a smile. Saif didn't know why this man was there. "Come and sit here on this pot," Humaid said to Saif. The big round tin pot was kept upside down and meant to act as a chair, where the boy's legs will be free from all sides.

"But, Grandpa, I don't want to cut my hair; I had it cut last week. Remember, you took me to the barber?" Saif said to his grandfather.

"Yes, Saif, I do remember, but this time Humaid is here for a different reason. Please, son, sit on the pot and look at the roof. I am with you. Don't be afraid," Saif's grandfather told him. Saif obeyed his grandfather and sat on the pot. Saif's grandfather came behind him, hugged him from the back, and held Saif's hands to his chest. He gave a wink for the barber to start. Saif saw all of this, but then his grandfather lifted his head up and told him, "What do you think of this roof, Saif?" Saif could sense his pants being pulled down, and he could feel the barber's cold hands reaching for his thing. He tried to move or escape, but his grandfather had him pinned on that pot like a nail on a piece of wood. He tried to scream, but he felt no pain since the barber used a local anesthetic on his penis. Then he felt a cotton bud wrapped around his penis and covered with a piece of cloth.

"It's all over. See, nothing to it," Humaid said with sarcasm.

"Happy circumcision, my boy," Grandpa told Saif. Grandfather went to collect his rifle and fired another three-gun shots in the air. "Let everyone know that our boy has entered manhood," Grandpa said with joy. Saif looked down and saw his thing wrapped in a piece of rag. The whole ordeal did not take a long time, but for him, it was like ages. He sat on the pot, staring down, with questions swirling in his head. *What is that word Grandpa used?* He couldn't even pronounce it, let alone remember it. Saif sat there trying to understand what had just happened. Not able to speak or even cry, he just sat there, staring downward. His grandfather sipped coffee with the barber, and then handed the barber one silver coin and ushered him out. Saif's mother came up the stairs. She looked at her boy with a smile, and then a drop of tear slid down her white cheeks.

"Thanks God it is over. How you are feeling, my boy?" She kissed Saif on his forehead. Saif did not answer.

His grandfather came back and addressed him, "Listen, Saif, we had to remove that piece of skin from your thing for cleansing purpose. The wound will heal in no time, but it will feel itchy for some time. Do not scratch it. If it persists, and you can't hold yourself from scratching, just take warm pieces of stone and keep over it until the itching goes away. Do you understand?"

Saif nodded his head in agreement. He tried to lift himself up from that pot, but felt that his legs are shacking. His mother came to help him. She put a pillow on the ground and asked him to sit on it. For one month, Saif endured the pain and itching in his penis, and his mother used to change the wound dressing every day after cleaning it. Eventually, the wound healed, and Saif was able to play and act normal again.

Mud House similar to Saif's house with room upstairs

Chapter Two

After learning how to read and write, Saif started learning math and how to deal with numbers. Since in his time there were no formal schools, his grandfather used to teach him either in the field or at home. Luckily, his grandfather had Abacas to aide Saif how to add and subtract. Saif knew that without good knowledge of reading, writing, and math, he would never be able to read the *"Book"* and would never know the secret of magic.

The stream that runs near his house always amazed him. With the water flowing endlessly from underground, down to irrigate the whole town, the birds that hover over it singing and flopping their wings, and the green grass growing along the banks of the stream, all seem to be a picture that an artist should capture. Water means life, and with that thought, Saif used to spend some time thinking about all the living creatures that survive on this stream while sitting on the stream bank. Humans use water, animals use water, and plants use water, but do Jin also use water? That question always haunted him; if they do, where do they get it from? How come he never saw them attending to the stream to take their needs of water? Yet if Jin exists, how come he never got to see them? Do Jin really exist, or are they just a myth in his grandfather's head? All these questions circled through Saif's head while watching the stream water gently flow, with the water sound playing its own kind of symphony. That stream's water sound sometimes made Saif drowsy, and he fell asleep on the grass on the stream bank.

Since Saif had become accustomed to visiting the stream, he decided to make a sanctuary for himself. He collected palm tree leaves and started building a small hut that will be his secret place whenever he needed a break or just a relaxing time. The neighbor boy, Khalfan, was passing by when he spotted Saif doing something and offered to help. Saif was not comfortable with Khalfan's offer, but when he saw the boy's sincerity, he forgot about the last quarrel he had with him and decided to give Khalfan a second chance. Besides the fact, he needed another helping hand to help him construct his humble hut. With the help of Khalfan, the two started erecting the palm tree trunks, which acted as columns, and covered the side and the roof with the palm tree leaves. Khalfan was the only boy neighbor that Saif knew. He lived two houses away from Saif's house, and he was about the same age. Though Khalfan worked in the field like Saif, he was not lucky enough to be taught since his father didn't know how to read or write. Saif started to teach his friend some of the basic education that he was getting from his grandfather, and that made the bond between the two fellows very strong. One thing that bothered Saif about Khalfan was that Khalfan did not share his passion for magic. As a matter of fact, Khalfan thought that there was no such thing as magic and always argued with his friends that one should not mess with the other worlds.

Hut similar to Saif's hut by the stream

The hut they built was enough to shelter them from the summer burning sun and to give them a safe place to practice their knowledge and dream about their future lives. In this hut, Saif started his own self-schooling; he used to sneak whatever books he could take from his grandfather's bookshelves and started reading them. Some books were religious books, some were stories, and some were poems, but none were about magic since his grandfather kept the magic books in a locked chest box, and he was the only one who had the key. All these books didn't seem to satisfy Saif's hunger for knowledge; he wanted more. More to open his mind to the outside world and broaden his knowledge. Khalfan used to take advantage of his friend's curiosity for knowledge and used to ask him to tell him some of the stories he had read. Saif used to tell the story to his friend, and it wasn't the story itself that amused his friend, but the way Saif told it. He used to change his voice whenever the characters in the story changed, but always had difficulty imitating women's voices, that's what made Khalfan laugh.

Saif's childhood was not that happy; it was tiresome, from helping his grandfather in the field to going to the local market trying to sell the field products and purchasing his family needs, to studying and getting an education. But night for him was a time of peace and tranquility. Night was so mysterious to Saif and he was so sacred that he spent hours and hours watching the sky or just laying down thinking of his world and the other worlds. One time, he dared to ask his mother a question that was bothering him.

"Mama, are there any worlds other than our world?" he asked. His mama was astonished and, yet she had to answer her young boy's question.

"Yes," his mother replied. "There are other worlds, beyond ours, but they have their own domain, which should not, in any means, affect our own world."

"Domain? What does that mean, mother?" Saif inquired.

"Well, that means, as the creator has created us to live in this land and facilitated things for us to live by, so he has done for the other worlds; they have their own space and time and living environment, which should not be mingled or mixed with our world, that what domain means, and be careful, my son," she added. "As we have our own world and we don't like others to intrude in our world, so do the other worlds; they don't like to be bothered by other species different than their species."

Saif was confused, and he had to ask his mother this question. "If we are not supposed to intrude into other worlds like Jin's for instance, then why is Grandpa doing it?" His mother didn't answer him and went on cleaning the house. Saif found it unnecessary to press his mother for an answer, but he would wait until his grandfather came home.

Saif waited that night for his grandfather anxiously to come home, but his grandfather didn't show up. He asked his mother about her father, and she told him that his grandfather had to go out of town to visit a relative who was sick and he would not be back that night. Saif had his dinner and went to his bed early, disappointed that he could not ask his grandfather the question that his mother declined to answer. Saif had a mixed feeling that night between what his mother had told him about the other worlds and what grandfather was doing. *If we are not supposed to interact with the Jin world, why does Grandpa do it? What benefit or pleasure does he get out of it? And the most important thing: how does he do it?* All these questions were making him sleepless and helpless. Saif was sleepless because his desire to see the other world was shattered and helpless because he still young to know all the facts. When Saif woke-up in the morning, he recited his prayer very quickly, put on his field dress, and ran out of the house. His mother was calling after him to eat his breakfast, but he was in a hurry and replied swiftly that he would eat in the field.

Saif was astonished to see his grandfather already working in the field. He was surprised because he knew that his grandfather was out of town, and he wasn't expecting him before end of the day since the trip from Saif's town to the relative's town took at least two days on animal's back or four days by foot. *How did Grandpa do it in less than one day?* The question kept hovering in his mind, and he was determined to ask. Saif embraced his grandfather and asked him how the sick man was. Grandfather replied, "He is much better after I treated him."

Then the boy asked, "Grandpa, how did you manage to go and come back this fast?"

Grandpa nodded his head and said, "It is all in the book, son, so let's continue working."

Saif worked in cultivating some of the ready palm fruits. With palm trees growing several meters above ground, they require great skills to climb and reach the fruits at the top. Now he was ten years old, and with the aid of his grandfather, Saif learned how to conquer his fear of height and how to climb the tree faster than a trained monkey. He slipped the rope past the right side of his waist, tied the rope around the tree, and knotted it back at the left side of his waist. Then firmly put his legs on the tree trunk with his two hands holding the rope and sliding it up the tree trunk until he reached the top. His grandpa, being old and physically unfit to climb, usually waited down to receive the cultivated fruit with another rope tangled from the top of the tree to the ground and a basket attached at its ground end. The grandfather would empty the content, give the basket a little shake, and Saif would understand the sign to start pulling the basket upward. This process took around half an hour for each tree, and Saif had to climb three more trees that day, so he didn't have much time to mingle with his grandfather. The view at the top of the tree was very different than the view from the bottom. At the ground level, everything seems so huge and big; his grandfather being tall and slim seemed like a giant in Saif's eyes. The trees and surrounding homes seemed to be very high in the sky, but at the treetop elevation, everything seemed so small and dwarfed. Saif could see the whole field and even some of the nearby houses. From up there, Saif's grandfather looked very small, especially since the tree trunk was so high, and he often wondered how such a creature could communicate with different worlds.

After finishing all three trees, he sat down with his grandfather to have a midday meal. The grandfather noticed that his grandson was thinking about something; he wanted to find out. "So, Saif, tell me, how is your reading going? Are you comfortable with the way I am teaching you?" Saif didn't answer since he was busy chewing the dates and drinking the milk. His grandfather did not persist on questioning him as he could see that Saif was very hungry and eating his meal like a hungry horse.

Saif realized that his grandfather asked him a question and that he did not reply, so he apologized to his grandfather and asked him to repeat the question again. Grandpa asked him the same two questions, and Saif replied, "My reading is improving very well, and even my math is getting better." He told his grandfather the story he encountered with the fruit seller in the market, where the fruit seller could not do the math properly and gave Saif more change money than he deserved, and how Saif explained to the man how to add and subtract numbers and returned the excess money back to him. His grandfather was very pleased, and tapped on his grandson's shoulder, saying, "You are growing up just fine."

"Grandpa," called Saif, "can I ask you a question?"

"Yes, son, go ahead," replied Grandpa.

"Every time you open the grand book, you mutter words that I don't understand. What is that language?" Saif addressed his grandfather.

"Well, you know, son, to everything there is time, and when the time is right, you will understand that language," his grandfather replied.

"Yes, yes…but is that Jin language?" Saif kept asking. "Do Jin exist, Grandpa? Can you see them? Can you talk to them?" Saif went on.

"Take it easy, my boy, as I told you, you will know everything at its own time, but for now, let's finish our work," his grandfather told him. While at their recess, a girl passed by and she waved hello to Saif's grandfather, then she lowered her head in shyness and went away.

Saif asked his grandfather, "Who is that girl?"

The grandfather replied, "Her name is Salma, and she is here to visit her grandmother."

"Her grandmother!" exclaimed Saif. "Which one?"

"Do you know Auntie Aza living at the end of our block?" his grandfather asked him.

Saif nodded. "Yes."

"This is her niece from another town. She came yesterday, and I met her in her grandmother's house when I visited them," Grandpa explained. Saif could not see the girl's face clearly, but he saw her petite body and nice figure and he started to imagine what she looks like. With no experience with the female gender, Saif seemed to be fascinated to meet the girl, and he asked his grandfather if he was going to visit them again. The grandfather told him, "Yes. Tonight, her grandmother has invited me to their house for dinner since I had helped them find their missing goats." Seeing the curiosity in the boy's eye, the Grandpa knew that his grandson wanted to join him, but not to embarrass him, he asked him, "Would you like to come?" Saif replied with an affirmative yes. The rest of that day, Saif was busy thinking how the night would be. What he was going to say to the girl when he first sees her – that is if he was allowed to see her. And how he should present himself? Well, time flies when one's mind is busy with something, and before Saif could notice, the night had spread its blanket in the area with its quietness and darkness. Saif rushed home to change and get ready to go with his grandfather. He requested his mother to give him his best dress and if she can manage, a small splash of perfume from his grandfather. His mother saw his enthusiasm, and she did not ask him since her father had already told her that he was taking the boy with him to have dinner at Auntie Aza's house. Yet she did not know that the boy was going on another mission rather than just being an escort. She did not know that her son could not stop thinking of that girl he saw at a glance that day, and that he was counting the minutes to see her again. Saif put on his best dress, got his cap and coat, dipped the perfume stick in the perfume jar, and rubbed that perfume on his body and clothes. He took a look at the mirror hanging on the wall, and smiled when he saw himself all set for the new endeavor. "Let's go, Saif; we don't want to be late," his grandfather called him, and swiftly he went along with his grandfather. Saif carried the kerosene lamp since the whole surrounding was very dark, and the only way to see the way was by holding a portable kerosene lamp. The moon was absent, and the tall palm trees stood on the side of the pathway like huge monsters with their black trunk and their concave leaves. They walked in silence; only the sound of the tree's branches hissing with the wind and the sound of the nocturnal insects could be heard. They arrived at Auntie Aza's house after a short trip. Grandpa knocked on the big carved wooden door with his stick, and the answer came, saying that somebody is on the way. Here Saif's heart started beating very fast; in one hand, he wished that the beautiful girl would open the door, but on the other hand, he wished that someone else would open the door so that he would have a better look at the girl in his own time. The door was opened by Auntie Aza herself, since she was expecting her guests to arrive and it is only polite to meet them at the door. Women are not supposed to shake hand with strange men, so she waved hello to Saif's grandfather and shook hand with Saif since he was still a boy and took the lamp from his hand. She welcomed them inside and led them to the sitting room. Aza was a wealthy lady; she inherited all her wealth after her husband passed away. Her house was the biggest in the neighborhood and stood taller than any other building. Inside the house, white gypsum decoration could be seen near the ceiling, and a huge lamp was hanging from the ceiling in the middle of the room. The roof was decorated with candle wood and painted in dark brown color. For a moment, Saif was astonished by the beauty of the house, and he forgot about the little girl. The guests were seated on white thick cushions and were offered dates with coffee. Saif looked around, but never said a word; he was anticipating seeing the girl. Grandpa and Aza chatted about life issues, and she thanked him once again for helping her find the missing goats. Then she turned to Saif and said, "Boy! You have grown since the last time I saw you. You look much taller and handsome." Saif blushed and did not know how to answer, instead he just smiled. Aza went on, addressing Saif. "Have you met my granddaughter?" she inquired. "She is about your age, and she just arrived in town; unfortunately, she took permission to go and visit our neighbor's daughter, but she will be back soon," Auntie Aza told him. Saif was a bit disappointed, but he refrained from commenting.

Saif's grandfather interrupted, saying, "Yeah, she passed by this morning, while we were in the field." Aza ordered the maid to prepare the dinner and requested both her guests to go in the dining room for their dinner. As the custom requires, she can't join men for meals and she waited in the living room. The meal was kept on the floor, with a red cloth spread underneath. Meat, roasted chicken, bread, some vegetables, and some fruits were spread out. In between the food, jugs with fresh juice and water were placed in a circle. Saif and his grandfather ate, and ate until they were both full. Grandpa started reciting prayers after they finished their meal and then called upon their host to inform her that they had finished. Aza appeared with a smile, and led her guest to the living room again.

"I hope that the food was alright?" she inquired.

"It was very delicious." Grandpa replied politely.

They went on chatting about the market and general living conditions. With that heavy meal, Saif's head became heavy and he started to yawn. Then Grandpa requested permission to leave, but Saif was still hoping that the girl would be back by this time. "It's getting late, and we better leave," said Grandpa. "Thank you very much for your hospitality, and may the almightily bless you and your family," he added.

Aza nodded her head and said, "You are more than welcome; you deserve all good things for your help." As they were leaving, Saif heard a footstep coming toward the main door, and suddenly the door was opened with two beautiful faces standing there, shining like the moon light. Salma and her friend were at the door, and Saif stood there open-mouthed, wondering what to say.

"Hello, uncle," the two girls said to Saif's grandfather, and they disappeared in the house. Saif, still stunned, forgot to take the lamp over from Auntie Aza.

Auntie Aza politely told him, "This will help you in the dark." She handed the lamp to Saif. Saif took the lamp and waved goodbye to Auntie Aza. Grandpa thanked Aza once again and wished her goodnight. On the way, Saif didn't say anything, and walked visualizing the beautiful face he had seen.

Grandpa broke the silence and asked Saif, "Did you enjoy the dinner?"

"Yes," Saif replied. Then Saif dared to ask his grandfather a strange question. "Grandpa, how come you never married after Grandma passed away?"

Grandpa replied, "I have not found the right women who will fill up your grandmother's space."

Saif, without thinking, said, "What about auntie Aza?"

"What about her?" Grandpa asked.

"I mean, why didn't she get married?"

"I don't know; maybe this question should be asked to her," Grandpa said to Saif. Saif reached home and went straight to bed without saying anything to his mother. In his bed, he laid down and went over the whole day's events until he sank into deep sleep.

Chapter Three

The next day, Saif woke up late since it was off day. Friday is the off day, where Saif doesn't have to go to the field and he can spend the time enjoying himself. Besides that, he is allowed to wake up later than usual in the morning. Saif got dressed and went by his friend, Khalfan's, house to join him for a dip in the stream. Khalfan came along with his clothes, and small basket with dates, a coffee bottle, and two coffee cups. The two headed to the stream, and left their belongings in their hut. They swam, chanted, raced, and played in the water until midday prayer time. Then they headed to the hut, where they changed their wet clothes and prayed. Khalfan also brought with him a poem book, which had all the poems written about love stories. Khalfan started reading some.

"Say to the beautiful in the black veil, what have you done to the religious man?"

Saif was listening until Khalfan finished the whole poem. Then Saif asked Khalfan, "What do you think of love? I mean, how do you know love?" Saif asked.

Khalfan said, "As far as I know, love is in every one of us. We all love our parents, we love our brothers and sisters, and so on."

"No," Saif interrupted. "I mean, a love between a man and a woman; when does it happen?" continued Saif.

"I don't know!" said Khalfan.

"Oh, come on, haven't you ever felt that kind of attraction between you and the opposite sex? I mean girls," Saif proclaimed.

"Well, I do fantasize about a girl I saw once in the market; it is kind of an uneasy feeling in my stomach; could that be love? And you? Why all of a sudden you are asking these big questions? Are you in love?" Khalfan joked.

Saif did not reply, but he went on, "If I fall in love, then I will write my own poems."

While they were discussing the poems, they heard footsteps coming their way, and very quickly they hid the book. Salma and her friend Fatima were passing by. Khalfan stood up and went to Fatima to say hello. "Hello, Khalfan, what are you doing?" Fatima asked.

"We are reading poetry books, would you like to join us?"

"No thanks, we are on our way to visit someone, but maybe on our way back if that is alright with Salma?" Fatima said. Salma looked down in shyness, and they went on. Saif could not believe what his friend had done and how dare he bring two strangers to their secret place, but when he realized that Salma would be there, he forgot about all the outrage he had for Khalfan and started organizing the place. They kept the wet clothes aside, cleaned the small mat on the floor, and put the coffee bottle on the back side.

"What do you want to do with them?" asked Saif.

"Oh, just chat and see if they know anything about love," said Khalfan. Saif was outraged; he didn't want girls to know about boy talk, and when Khalfan saw his anger, he calmed him down and told him, "Don't worry, your secret is in deep well; I was just trying to pull your legs."

The girls came straight to the hut, and Khalfan invited them in, but Fatima said sorry they couldn't stay. "I have a proposal for you, Khalfan," said Fatima.

"What is it?" inquired Khalfan.

"Well, you know that we girls are not allowed to get education, but my friend and I are dying to know how to read and write, and we want you to teach us reading and writing," said Fatima.

"That is not a problem, but how do we do that without getting caught?" answered Khalfan.

"I have an idea," said Salma, who spoke for the first time. "I have learned how to weave palm tree leaves and make nice products with them. We will weave these leaves whenever anybody approached the hut, and get education whenever we feel it is safe."

"No one will suspect anything, and many boys and girls work together weaving these leaves; at the end, people will look at the final products," she went on.

Saif was very impressed by her idea and said, "Yes, we can make all sorts of baskets, date sacks, and even ropes; we will sell them in the local market and share the money to by slate and chalks."

"When will we have the time to do this?" asked Khalfan.

"Usually, we finish our work in the field by afternoon prayer, and then we have time until dusk," said Saif.

"We will take permission from our family to come and help you weave the leaves," said Salma.

"In the morning, we will gather the leaves, soak them overnight in water, and pile them nicely for weaving," Fatima went on.

"Starting tomorrow, we will meet here, and whoever gets here first should start working and pretend to be busy," said Saif. "Until tomorrow then?" The two girls waved goodbye and left.

The two boys brought camel shoulder bones, which they usually used as a slate, and some grounded charcoal mixed in water to act like ink kept in a jar, which was used instead of chalks. "We will use this for the time being, until we can afford a proper wooden slate and chalks," said Saif.

"You teach them reading and writing, and I will teach them math," said Khalfan. The next afternoon, the boys and the girls met in the hut. The girls came with the palm date leaves, and the boys brought their books hidden under their clothes.

"OK, we are ready, let's start," said Salma. Saif showed them the first letter in the alphabet, and quickly Salma weaved the same letter shape.

"That is very impressive," said Khalfan.

"Well, you have to know how to cross-weave these leaves, and you can make any shape you want," said Salma.

"That will make it easy for you now to write in the book," said Saif. "Here we go, you hold the straw like this, then dip it in the ink and start writing the first letter," Saif explained. He wrote the letter in big font on the bone slate using charcoal ink and the girls wrote in their books with straw and ink. "Good, now do that several times until you get used to it; meanwhile, we will start preparing these leaves so you can show us how to weave them," said Saif.

After the girls finished, they showed the boys how to weave the leaves.

"Depending on the shape you want to make, for a small basket, you use six leaves to start with in a "V" shape, three at each side, but for big sacks, one has to use twelve leaves, six at each side. To start, hold the leaves on "V" shape like this at the bottom of your hand, and then start folding them around each other, like this, until they become cross-knotted. You go on inserting leaves whenever you feel that the leaf tip is getting smaller," explained Salma. Saif and Khalfan tried but failed the first time. Salma showed them again, and Saif managed to get it around while Khalfan knitted everything in one knot, and they all started laughing at him. Khalfan did not lose hope and started all over again, until he finally got it.

"Boy! This is harder than learning how to read and write," he commented. This went on, the boys learning how to weave and the girls learning how to write and read.

Within the first week, the first basket was done, and the boys sold it at the local market. The four became very comfortable with each other; they started sharing their secrets and their dreams for the future. "Operation Cover-up," as they called it, had borne its fruits, and both teams were winners. The boys learned a new trade that brought them some nice income, and the girls now knew how to write, read, and do simple math. As time passed, the bond between them grew stronger. Saif usually admired anything that Salma did. He admired her smile, her small laughter, even her dress and the way she smelled. While Khalfan could not hide his passion for Fatima, and one time he told her that when he gets older, he will come and marry her!

Months passed by, and both the boys and girls got comfortable in the afternoon meeting, chatting, and spending the time of their lives. One summer afternoon, the four of them were suddenly faced with Auntie Aza standing in front of the hut with a very sad face; luckily, that time they were knitting the big date sack with domestic ropes and a big needle, but everybody guessed that Auntie Aza had bad news from the look of her face. Auntie Aza requested the girls to go with her to the house, and when Salma inquired, she told her that she got news that she would share with her at home. Later that afternoon, Saif and Khalfan learned that Salma's mother had passed away, and Auntie Aza was wise to inform Salma calmly at home. Saif didn't know what to do, and he informed his grandfather about Salma's loss. His grandfather traveled to Salma's hometown to give his condolences, and when he came back, he informed Saif that Salma would stay there for some time. Saif thought of writing Salma a letter expressing his sorrow for her loss, but he didn't know how to send it. Then he thought of Fatima, and maybe there was a way of communication between the two girls. Fatima told him that she would visit Salma within a few days, and she would be happy to secretly give her the letter. Saif sat down early in the morning and started writing.

My dearest Salma, deep down in me, I feel that your loss is mine. I know how it feels to miss somebody. I have never got to see my father and now I will miss seeing the ray of light that shine from your cheeks. My comfort is that I know that you will be back, and we will continue our meeting. Please take care of yourself and come back soon.

Dearest Yours,
Saif.

Fatima secretly took the letter to her friend while she was visiting her. Salma read the letter, and a drop of tear flowed from her eyes. Fatima teased her. "Is it love? You can tell me, and you know I will keep your secret." Salma could not answer her, and she kept quiet. Before Fatima left the next day, Salma handed her a small paper, and she asked her to give it to Saif. Fatima took the letter and gave it to Saif, whom she found working in the field. Saif took the letter and went underneath a big tree to read it.

My dear Saif, thank you for the sympathy and great condolences you have conveyed through your last letter. I don't know how to tell you this news, but it tears me apart that I will not be able to see your beautiful smile, or your handsome looks any more. My uncle has decided that I will stay with him since, you know, both my parents are gone. Oh dear! I will cherish every moment we spent together and will always look forward to seeing you again, but for now, please take care.

Your friend,
Salma.

Saif became very sad and gloomy, and he looked for his friend, Khalfan, to tell him that "Operation Cover-up" no longer existed. So, he headed toward Khalfan house, but unfortunately no one was home. Then he went to the field to see if he could spot Khalfan anywhere, but Khalfan was nowhere to be found. Tired and dizzy, Saif decided to head to the hut. When he entered, he saw Khalfan lying inside. "Where have you been?" Saif asked him.

"I got tired of work, and I came to take a nap here," replied Khalfan. "Why? What happened?" inquired Khalfan. Saif told him that he received a letter from Salma and that she was not coming, which meant that their project is dead. Khalfan felt sorry but kept quiet and continued his nap.

Chapter Four

There was a heavy knock on the house door. Grandpa requested Saif to go and see who was it. "Saif, go and see who is at the door," Grandpa said. Saif went and saw a tall man breathing heavily and looking very tired.

"Is your grandfather home?" asked the strange man.

"Yes, whom shall I tell him is asking?" Saif replied.

"Please tell him that I need to speak to him very urgently; I need his help," the strange man said.

"Saif, let the man in," said Grandpa. "Why you keeping him at the door? Take him into the living room; I will be there soon." Saif ushered the strange man in and led him to the living room. He sat with him until Grandpa arrived. "Hello, my dear, how are you?" Grandpa greeted the man. "Please be seated," said Grandpa. Grandpa asked the man where he came from, and how were the people there, and how he could help him.

The man said, "I came here seeking your help, and I know that you can." The man went on, "I came from the nearby village to buy some commodities from the market, and my town people, when they learned that I was heading to the market, they asked me to help them buy some spices that they would use for the upcoming celebration. Everyone gave me some coins and asked me to buy them the required quantity of spices. I took the money and registered everyone's requirements on a piece of paper so that I would not mix them up or forget when I reached to the shop. On the way, I stopped to have a meal along with a shepherd, whom I had met on the way. We ate together, and then I bid him farewell before heading to the market. To my astonishment, when I reached the market, I searched for the money in the sack which I had put in, but the money was nowhere to be found. I went back to the place where I had the meal with the shepherd and looked for the money; perhaps it had fallen there unnoticed, but no luck. Then I went to the shepherd's house and asked him if he had seen the money, but he denied it. Now I am here, and I need your help to get the money." The strange man completed his story.

"Don't worry. Go back to the market, and the shepherd will give you the money there," Grandpa said to the strange man. "Go on, and have no worries," said Grandpa. Saif was following this story like watching a movie in a theater, and he was wondering how his grandfather knew that the Shepherd had taken the money. The man asked to be excused and went on his way. Saif asked his grandfather how he knew where to find the money, and Grandpa told him, "Come closer, and I will teach you."

"See, in each of us there is a companion whom we can neither see nor feel. God has gifted me with a talent and that I can communicate with my companion, who in turn can communicate with any other companion in a psychic way and through learning some technique. When the man started telling his story, I asked my companion to get in sync with

Shepherd's companion and see if he had taken the money. The signal I got was that the shepherd was lying, and he did indeed take the money. With my influence, I managed to instruct his companion to plant guilt in the shepherd's heart and scare him, and I told him that he would face severe consequences if the money did not return to its rightful owner. That's how I got to know that the shepherd would voluntarily return the money, and I bet he has returned it by now," Grandpa said, sharing everything.

"But, Grandpa, where did you learn this technique?" asked Saif.

"It is all in the book, which I intend to teach you now that you have joined adulthood. There are a few rules you have to adhere to before you start reading the book. Rule number one: you have to be clean before touching the book, rule number two: never try to harm anyone with what's written in the book nor try to influence any personal benefit for yourself by exploiting some of the secrets that you will be discovering, and finally, the most important rule is, never tell anyone about your secret. Now if you promise me that you will be following these rules, then I will start teaching you the secrets of the Book," Grandpa concluded his talk. Saif knew that his grandfather was very sincere in wanting him to get to know the trade.

"I promise you, Grandpa, that I will stick to all those rules," Saif told his grandfather.

Friday morning, Saif and his grandfather had their breakfast at home, and then grandfather opened his chest box where he kept the Book. He took the book out, which was wrapped in red velvet cloth, and recited some words. "See, this book is divided into four sections," he started explaining. "The first section is in Astrology Science, the science of the stars," he explained. "Here, the horoscope circle is the most important thing to understand, which I will explain to you later. Then, the second section is on how to find lost items, the third section is on people relations; and last, but not least, is how to master communication with other worlds. I want you, for the time being, only to learn the first three sections, and the fourth, you can only learn after I depart this earth. The last section is so powerful that if you attempted to go over it without proper preparations, it might harm you. I will teach you the technique for approaching the last section, but no one, and I stress no one, should be around you when you start reciting that last section, do you understand?" Grandpa asked Saif.

"Yes, Sir, I do understand," replied Saif.

"OK, with that in mind, every Friday, we will read some parts of the book until you master most of its secrets," said Grandpa. Saif took the book in his lap, and he felt a heavy load had just been set on his body, even though the book does not weigh that much, yet he felt its weight nailing him to the floor beneath him. He flipped through the first few pages and then started reading loudly. His grandfather interrupted him and instructed him to read with a humming noise that came out of the nose; no word should come out clear from his mouth, like this, and Grandpa started making the humming noise, which, long ago, Saif thought was a foreign language. Saif followed, but he had great difficulty getting the words out of his nose, so difficult that he started sneezing. "You will get used to it," Grandpa told him. "Just keep practicing." Saif went on reading very slowly, but he didn't seem to understand a word of what he was reading, yet he went on. "You will not understand many things at first time, but once I explain it to you, you will find it interesting," his grandpa told him. "First of all, you may have noticed that this book is handwritten in cursive handwriting, and as you can see, some of the letters are hard to distinguish, add to that, some of the words are broken into several letters. So, you have to make sense of what you are reading by understanding the word location, and what purpose it serves," Grandpa went on. "To make it easy for you, you will read one full sentence, and then I will explain any ambiguity in it, OK?" said Grandpa.

"Sure," answered Saif. So he went on reading, the different geographical directions, and Grandpa explained to him where North, South, East, and West are. Then he came across the different names of the stars and planets and the different names of galaxies and their pathways. They went on until noon prayer, then quit reading and went to pray.

Saif didn't spend his spare time in the hut with his friend, Khalfan, like he used to be, and that made Khalfan wonder why Saif was avoiding his company! Saif explained to Khalfan that now that his grandfather is getting old, he needs somebody to help him around the house. Khalfan told his friend, "Why didn't your grandpa get married? This way, he will get all the help around the house, and you and I could spend our time like before."

"Good idea; why didn't I think of that?" said Saif. "But who will agree to marry such an old man?" Saif asked.

"I know just the right person, but you will have to help me first convince your grandpa to agree, in principle, with the marriage idea," said Khalfan.

"I will open the subject to him once I have a chance," said Saif. "But whom do you have in mind?" he inquired.

"Auntie Aza, yes Auntie Aza, she is the most appropriate lady for him; she is almost his age, barren, and your grandpa can easily live with her," said Khalfan. Saif thought of what Khalfan had proposed, and it did make sense, except for one thing: his mother and he will be a lone if Grandpa leaves. "I think you are right, but who will be with my mother after Grandpa leaves? I mean, my mother will be alone, unless…?"

"Unless what?" asked Khalfan.

"Nothing; forget it," said Saif.

"No, no, tell me, because I am also thinking of something," went on Khalfan. "I think I should also get married; that's what I was thinking, but I feel it is a stupid idea; I mean, I am barely eighteen years old," said Saif.

"Exactly, my thinking, and I think you know your bride!" said Khalfan.

"Yeah, I know," said Saif, and drifted off into his dreams. He went on to imagine what it would be like to be married. Did his dream girl share his passion? Will he be a good husband and a good parent? And will love be their common denominator? Saif woke up with a swift hand blow from Khalfan to the tip of his head.

"Let's go, dream boy, and break the news to your mother first, because she has a better influence on her father. Beside the fact that the idea will be more acceptable to your grandpa if your mother is convinced." They both headed to Saif's home.

Saif found his mother in the house, getting ready to prepare lunch, when he walked in with his friend, Khalfan.

"Mother, we need to talk to you about an important subject," said Saif.

"Sure, my child," said Saif's mother.

"Well, you know that Grandpa is getting old, and he needs someone to assist him and take good care of him. I know, Mother, that you are doing the best you can, but still, I think someone more intimate or a soul mate will be more helpful," said Saif.

"Simply what Saif is trying to say is that he wants to get married, but he also will be happy if his grandfather will also get married first," jumped in Khalfan.

"Well, that is great news, my boys, but I think not only two, but also, you, Khalfan, should get married," said Saif's mother.

"See what you got yourself into, Khalfan. Well done, Mama; we all will marry in one night," joked Saif.

"So where is the problem, and who are the proposed brides?" asked Saif's mother.

"Auntie Aza, her niece Salma, and our neighbor Fatima," spoke Khalfan very quickly.

"I understand the part about Auntie Aza for my father, but who is getting whom of the other two?" inquired Saif's mother.

"I will marry Salma, and Khalfan is deeply in love with Fatima," said Saif. They all laughed and Saif told Khalfan, "I was just pulling your legs."

"Do you think Grandpa will agree to this proposal?" Saif asked his mother.

"Leave my father to me; I know how to convince him. Besides, I need to know from the ladies if they will agree to their proposed future grooms," said Saif's mother. "I will open the subject today with my father, and then I will have ladies talk with Auntie Aza to have her feedback on this plan. Once everything is ready, I will tell you boys to formally go along with your grandfather and other dignitaries for a formal proposal. Let me cook this one nicely, or else you will have no marriage and no lunch today," said Saif's mother. They all laughed, and Khalfan left for his home anxiously, waiting for the good news.

At night, Saif's mother approached her father and told him that Saif had now become ready for marriage and that she had opened the subject with him, but he said he didn't want to leave him alone. Grandpa smiled, and then he said, "Do you want me to talk to him?"

"No, he had a better idea," she said.

"Oh, he has? And what is that?" Grandpa asked.

"He wants you and his friend, Khalfan to get married with him," Saif's mother said. Grandpa smiled and he kept silent.

"Khalfan is still young, but who will agree to marry an old man like me?" said Grandpa in sarcasm.

"Leave that to me; you just have to agree to the idea, and I will do the rest," said Saif's mother.

"May God do what is best," her father told her.

Saif's mother went to visit Auntie Aza's house the next day. Aza welcomed her guest very warmly, and after chit chat and small talk, Saif's mother told Aza how highly her father speaks of her and that he wishes her the best. Then she told her that he was feeling lonesome and another mate would make his life easier. That's when Aza's face blushed. "I am here requesting your permission to tell my father to come formally and request your hand from your family. I know that this will make my father very happy and will give him such an excellent companion," Saif's mother went on.

"May God do whatever is best," she replied.

"Now that I have got your permission for my father, my son also is seeking your niece's hand, and from the bottom of my heart, I hope that you will agree," said Saif's mother.

"I don't have a say in my niece's marriage. That is for the men to decide, but as far as I know, the two will make a cute couple," Aza said.

"Well, then we manage to hit two birds with one stone, or as they say, only one more mission is left," said Saif's mother.

"And what is that?" asked Aza.

"Khalfan and Fatima. They also want to get married. Khalfan's mother promised me that she would speak to Fatima's mother and inform me of the outcome. Once they agree, then a formal wedding will be announced," said Saif's mother.

"Best of luck," said Aza. Khalfan told his friend, Saif, that Fatima's family had no objection to him proposing to marry her. The wedding was set within one week.

Old Mud houses

Chapter Five

The wedding was conducted on Monday night with full moonshine, based on the recommendation of Saif's grandfather. "Monday is a lucky day; all the stars are revealing that prosperous days are ahead," Grandpa told Saif and Khalfan, and they both agreed. The young brides were escorted to Saif's and Khalfan's houses, accompanied by singing, folk dancing, and yodeling. For Grandpa and his bride, there was no celebration; merely, Grandpa shifted his belongings to Aza's house one day ahead, and the religious ceremony was conducted on Monday with a small gathering of dignitaries and religious people. For the youngsters, the brides dressed in green dresses and were covered from head to toe with white veil. Since the two grooms lived close to each other, their brides were escorted together. They started from Aza's house and walked the distance to the groom's house. Both grooms were dressed up well for the occasion, and each one held a sword in his hand. At Saif's house, Salma was taken to the room upstairs, where Saif waited patiently for his bride; the room where Saif first entered manhood, and now he was about to step into a holy matrimonial life. Two old servant ladies entered the room with Salma to help here with her veil and to make sure that

Salma was comfortable. Saif received his bride with a smile, and he knew that Salma could see it, but he still could not see hers since her face was covered. The two sat close to each other. Saif took Salma's hand and started saying his prayer. Thanking his Lord for this blessing and hoping that the upcoming days were full of joy and happiness. Then he pulled the veil from his bride's face, which was shining like the moon shining outside. Very gently, he kissed her cheeks and gave a swift signal for the other two servant ladies to leave. Khalfan was also sitting anxiously waiting for Fatima, and when the two servant ladies ushered her in, Khalfan's heart started beating heavily with joy. Fatima could not hide her happiness either and decided to take the veil out on her own. Khalfan rushed to her, grabbed her from the two escorted ladies, and slammed the door, prohibiting anyone from entry. He took his bride and carried her like a baby in his arms, over the bed, and sank in his ocean of love. The next day morning, all three grooms met at the town hall, where a big festival was conducted in their honor. Saif stood near his grandfather, and Khalfan stood with his father to greet the well-wishers and usher them inside. The feast was rice with meat, and people sat in circles and got served as and when arrived. After finishing their meals, the well-wishers again wished each groom the best of luck and departed. This continued until noon, after which all three grooms were very tired and headed home to their brides.

Saif's grandfather came every Friday morning to Saif's house and continued teaching him about the book. He taught him astrology, human behavior, and most of all, how to interact within his inner self. "Close your eyes, and imagine that you can reach your companion with these simple words," and he told the words, "Do not think about the outside world, just you and your companion." Saif's grandfather told his nephew. Saif did what his grandfather told him, but got distracted by the image of Salma appearing in front of him every time he tried to concentrate. "Can you feel anything?" his grandpa asked, and Saif could not reply. "Can you feel anything, boy?" Saif's grandfather shouted, and by that time, Saif opened his eyes and said to his grandfather.

"I can only feel love, Grandpa," he said with a devilish smile on his face. The grandfather was stunned and could not say anything.

After a long silence, he asked him, "What do you mean you can only feel love?"

"Every time I close my eyes, I see the smiling face of my Salma. I try not to visualize her, but her image is just there. Sorry, Grandpa, let's try again," Saif added.

Grandpa smiled and said, "OK, but this time keep, Salma a side, and I will teach you how to connect with your companion, this is very important," insisted Grandpa. Saif closed his eyes, and with words coming out of his nose, he could feel a heavy load just landing on him. He was no longer in this world, and he could see crispy clear. He could see as far as he wanted. He could see wherever he wanted. He did not say a word; he just felt elevated, and he could see whatever he fancied. Yes, there was Salma sitting in front of the mirror, combing her hair, and rhyming a little love song. He could see his mother busy in the kitchen, and he could see birds hovering over the corn field. *This is unbelievable. I really can see with my heart whatever my eyes can't see,* Saif thought joyfully. With a pinch from his grandpa on his cheeks, he opened his eyes. "Well, boy, how was it?" his grandfather inquired.

"It was fantastic, Grandpa. It is an indescribable feeling; I really felt that I was outside this world," Saif explained.

"Well, I taught you how to get to that state, but I have to teach you how to come out of it," his grandfather said. "As you have recited some words to get to that state, you have to say the same words, but backward, to get out." Grandpa went on telling him how to transform a word by reading it backward. Saif recited the words after his grandfather, and it sounded funny since the words were not familiar to him. "The only way to memorize these words is to write them in their correct form, then write them in their backward form," Grandpa told Saif. Saif nodded his head in abeyance.

While in their session, they heard a heavy knock on the main door. Grandpa asked Saif to answer the door and see who was there. Saif went to the door and was greeted by an old lady who asked him, "Is your grandfather here, because I went to Aza's house and they told me that he is here."

Saif said, "Yes, he is here, but he is busy now."

"Please tell him that I need him on an urgent matter," the old lady replied. Saif went to his grandfather and told him that an old lady was demanding to see him for an urgent matter. Grandpa told him to let her in. The lady came in and greeted Saif's grandpa and he returned the greeting.

"What can I do to help you?" Grandpa asked.

"I need your help to find a missing gold ring," the lady started. "This ring has been in my family for a long time, and yesterday, while looking in my chest box, I could not find it. I looked everywhere, searched each place in the house and I could not trace it. I am sure that someone has taken it, because a few days ago, I checked and it was there," she went on telling her story.

"Does anyone beside you have a key to the chest?" Grandpa asked.

"No, but of late, I had hired a servant to come and clean the house in the morning. She is a decent lady, and I have known her for a long time. The key is always with me, I have made a necklace and I hang it around my neck," she added. Saif was listening to all of this conversation, and he started his ritual inner self communication, while his grandpa, watching, pretended to ignore him.

"Are there any other items missing from the chest beside the ring?" Grandpa asked.

"No, only the ring. It is the most valuable item, and what surprised me is that all items are in place without disturbance, which means whoever has done it was not in a rush," the old lady went on. Saif, now in his new state, could see very clearly what had happened and who took the ring.

He snapped out and muttered, "I know who took your ring."

"Sorry, my boy, I could not hear you."

"I know who took the ring, I said," Saif spoke loudly this time. "While you were taking a shower, you left the key to the chest on the small wall inside your bath along with your dirty clothes, and you requested the maid to take the dirty clothes and bring you new, clean ones from your room. While taking the dirty clothes from the bath, the maid discovered that she also had taken the chest key. She went in the room, opened the closet to bring you a clean dress, and it was unlocked. She did not know that the key was for the chest, but when she found the wardrobe unlocked, she knew that this key could only be for the chest. She opened the chest box, pretending to fetch the other dress, and she slipped the ring in her bra and locked the chest and came out. She placed the new clothes and the key where it was so you would not suspect anything. The ring is with the maid," Saif went on. Grandpa was impressed and the woman was stunned because she came for the old man's salvation and she was rescued by the young man.

"Is that true?" she asked Grandpa.

"Every word of it," replied Grandpa. "And don't worry, when you go back home, you will find the ring on the small wall in your bathroom where you left the key."

"I am sure I will since the maid came and said she was sick and she couldn't help me today." The old lady asked to be excused and Saif went with her to the doorstep.

Grandpa was very proud of what Saif had learned and he told him, "You are a very clever and a quick learner." Saif could not hide his happiness at his grandfather's compliment and sat down to continue the lesson. Another knock on the door disturbed them again, and Saif went up immediately to open the door.

A small boy stood there. He said to Saif, "My mother wants to thank you and your grandfather. She got her ring back after the maid admitted of taking it, and my mother is sending these two silver coins for your grandfather."

Saif took the money from the boy and gave it to his grandfather, but his grandfather gave the money back to him, saying, "This is your first earning." Saif took the money with a cheerful smile and went with his grandfather to answer the call for the Friday prayer.

Stream with Palm trees on its banks

Chapter Six

Now, Grandpa was getting old. Besides the fact he was married to a wealthy lady, he was also not attending the field with Saif. Saif was now strong enough to handle all the field work on his own and share the crops with his grandfather. Whatever he gained from the field, he split into three shares: one for his grandfather's house, one for his house, and one share he sold in the market. People started to know that Saif had acquired the trade of magic from his grandfather, so people used to flock to his house, seeking healing from sickness, trying to find lost items, or even making love amulets for their beloved women. Saif was always busy, either in the field or at home. Some people went to the field when they couldn't find him at home, and some people knocked on his door even at midnight. The knock came very strong on this one cold night. Saif thought of ignoring it, since he was tired and didn't want someone to disturb him. But the knock continued, and he forced himself to go and find out who was this lunatic knocking on the door like that at this time of night.

He opened the door and saw his friend, Khalfan, in front of him. "Oh, it's you," he said to Khalfan. Khalfan embraced his friend and told him, "Please, come with me.

Your grandfather has passed away." Saif could not let his friend go and grabbed him closer while tears were dripping from his face. Khalfan stood there until Saif let go. Saif went inside the house and woke up his mother and wife, and told them the sad news. His mother started crying, and Salma also wept beside her.

"There is no time for this now; we must go to Auntie Aza's house," Saif commanded. They went along with Khalfan to Aza's house and found Grandpa lying on the bed with cold feet and hands. Saif kissed his grandpa cheeks and stood beside his wife. Saif's mother, Aza, and Salma left the room, and other men came to take the body. Saif's grandfather's body was taken to a funeral house, where the body was washed and rubbed with perfume, and then covered with a single piece white cloth. Prayers were said for the body and the body was taken to the cemetery for burial. All the town men came for the funeral, and the body was taken on the shoulder of four people to the cemetery. At the graveyard, the body was lowered down in the grave and buried. Saif was so sad for losing his grandfather, but what to do, this was life. For three days, Saif administered his grandfather's condolences. People came from everywhere; some of them came from the other towns, and Saif has to make arrangements for their lodging and food. The town people helped him, and his friend, Khalfan, was beside him all the time. Aza, now a widow, couldn't leave the house for four months and ten days, unless an emergency compelled her to do so. She stayed at home along with Saif's mother and wife and Saif used to split the time between taking care of his house and Aza's house.

Things were getting very busy with Saif, but something was bothering him more than other – the last chapter of the Book. He wanted to attempt to read it, but he remembered his grandfather advice that he had to be ready physically and mentally. He went on with his daily chores and days passed until one day he decided that it was time to discover the other world. He sat on his voyage, and made sure that his family had enough supply and money in case he did not come back. He did not reveal to his wife his intention, nor did he mention anything to his mother. He told his family that he had to go and visit a friend in another town and that his journey might take a week. The only one who knew about his tenure was his friend, Khalfan, and Saif had sworn him not to tell a soul.

"I will be going to a place outside the town, where I will be alone and can read the final chapter of the Book," he told Khalfan. "I want you to swear with your life that no one – and I mean no one – knows about this. The only reason I am telling you this is in case I do not make it back within one week, then you would know where to find me," Saif told his friend. Khalfan requested his friend to go with him, but Saif refused. "It is too dangerous; besides, if anything happens to me, you will know."

Saif spent the time preparing for his journey. He packed his meals, took out lodging material, and sat on his voyage to the unknown. He said farewell to his wife and mother and told them if ever they needed anything, they could take from Khalfan.

He traveled on the back of his donkey for three days, until he reached his destination. The place he had chosen was between the mountains and deserted. It was hard to be

alone in day time and scarier at night time, but Saif was
determined to go on.

Chapter Seven

Saif took his book out and kept it near him. He washed himself with the water he had taken and started with the secret words that his grandpa had taught him to open the book and that would guard him from any harm. This book had become to Saif more than a companion. He knew every page, every sentence, and every word except for the final chapter, which he had not attempted to read. Flipping through the pages, he reached the final chapter. His hands started sweating and shaking. He tried to hold the book tightly to his lap, but his hands still shook. He attempted to lift the book in the air and he couldn't, so he sat the book on the mat he was sitting on. He then stood up and walked away from the book, his hands now returning to normal. He went again and started to read the last chapter, but he couldn't, since his hands were shaking again. He left the book and walked around it. He came back, and this time he was determined not to let anything stop him from reading the last chapter. He took the book in both hands, placed it on his lap, and started reading. Every time he read a line, he felt his senses were getting heavier and heavier. He went on reading line by line, and the ground underneath him started shaking like a speedy train getting outside its track. It felt like an earthquake had just hit the ground and that the ground would open up and swallow him. He went on reading line by line and page by page until the last line when he felt a strong wind had lifted him up and he was no more in control of his senses. He closed his eyes to the force carrying him away. He could only hear the roaring around him, but he didn't know where he was heading and lost sense of all directions. Finally, the roaring stopped, and he could feel the ground beneath him again. Very slowly, he opened his eyes and to his astonishment, he was no longer in the deserted place he was in. He was now in different place, sitting underneath a big tree. All things around him were different in color, shape, and even smell. The trees had shaded leaves of all sorts of colors. The landscape was endless, and everything moved in the air. The only creature with legs in this place was Saif. He stood up and looked around him. *"This is definitely not my world; this is the Jin world,"* he thought to himself.

"Saif, Saif," the caller was calling. Saif could hear the voice, but he could not see anyone.

"Who is this? And where are you?" Saif called.

"I am up here," the caller replied.

"Up where?" Saif asked.

"Here," the caller answered. All that Saif could see was a small black smoke over his head, just like a bee hive, but no real shape or picture.

"I still can't see you, and all I can see is this black bee hive," Saif said.

"Well, that's me, and I can be in any shape you like to see me. So just tell me how you want to see me and I will transform," the caller answered.

"Can I see you in a human shape?" Saif asked. He looked near him, and there stood a middle-aged man.

"Welcome to our world," the man greeted Saif. "We have been waiting for your arrival ever since your grandfather passed away," he went on.

"Who are you?" Saif asked.

"I am your guardian and companion. I was with your grandfather before and now that he has left, I will be with you," the man told Saif. "I know this is your first time here, and things are very different from your world, but once you get accustomed to it, you will like it."

The man asked Saif to follow him.

"First, tell me, is this real or am I dreaming? Second, where are we going?" Saif asked the companion.

"This is real in this world, and you are not dreaming. We have to go and meet the others," replied the companion.

"The others?" Saif inquired.

"Yes, they are all aware that you are coming, and they want to appoint you as our leader whom we call Sheikh El Jin," the companion explained. The companion drew a line on the ground and asked Saif to cross it. Saif crossed the line and appeared in a vast room where everyone stood, waiting to greet him. The companion explained to him that they all appeared as human so he would be able to communicate with them very easily. "But don't be surprised if in the future you might see them in different shapes," he told him. Saif greeted each and every one of them and then he was asked to be seated at the head of the seating arrangement. He sat there and listened.

"Greetings to our new sheikh," an old man stood up and started to speak. "As with our late Sheikh, we are looking forward to your wise leadership, and all of us are honored that you are among us today. You know that our world is slightly different than yours, but we can use the human wisdom in sorting out some of our issues and we always need the guidance of the human teaching in religious matters, which our world lacks. We simply want you to be our leader, someone we can turn to in order to solve complicated issues that our doctrine has no real solutions for. For instance, the intervention of other human in our world and their insistence on mingling with our society with no definite aim. We need a human who can prevent them from entering our world and who can communicate with them the danger of pursuing such matters." The old man coughed and then went on, "We trusted your grandfather with our lives, and we welcomed him to our society because we knew he was the right man for this mission. Now we hope that you will carry this burden on your shoulder, and we will provide you with any assistance you require." The old man went on, "All of us here are at your service as long as you serve us with honor, dignity, and truth," the man directed his talk to Saif. "Now if you accept this ranking, we will swear you in as our leader, and if you decline, then we will parish you from this world, and you may not come again." Saif sat there, astonished, and did not speak a word. "So do you, Saif, swear that you will be our Sheikh as long as you live and honor this commitment?" the old man asked. Saif did not reply. The companion squeezed him heavily and told him to answer.

"Yes, I will honor my grandfather's commitment and accept to be your Sheikh," Saif said.

Saif looked around him, and all the people that were there had disappeared except for his companion. "What just happened?" he inquired.

"Once you have accepted your title, they all go to their original nature. You got to remember that those humans you were seeing were not humans, but they appeared in this way so you can recognize them and communicate with them easily. Now you will see them everywhere, in any shape you can imagine, and you will be able to recognize them and communicate with them." The companion went on addressing Saif, "We will be with you wherever you are; you will see us day and night, in your house, in the street, and every corner you can think of." The companion went on, and Saif was listening very carefully. "See, once you read the Book, and you come to our world, and once you accept the commitment of being our leader, you are like one of us; even though you are human, you will sense us everywhere."

Saif interrupted the companion. "And what do I get in return for all of this?" he asked.

"You will get our protection from any enemy, either human or otherwise, who will try to harm you. We cannot stop your fate from happening, but we will warn you ahead of time of any expected danger. Besides that, we will help you in your world in helping others. One thing you have to know, that we will not help you in any wrongdoing, and we don't expect you to ask for it," the companion explained. "So next time you see a stray cat, or a poor dog barking in front of your door, there is a chance that it might be one of us asking for guidance or help," the companion elaborated. "But you will know," he added. Saif just sat there and tried to digest all of this information that had landed on his head like a heavy rain. He had imagined such a different world, but he did not expect such a huge responsibility. *"In my world, I had enough problem of my own to be sorted out, and now that I burden the responsibility of another world. Will I be able to cope with this entire load?"* he asked himself.

"It is time for you to go back, and remember that we are with you all the time," the companion told Saif.

"And how do I go back?" Saif asked.

"Well, from now on, you just have to seek us out in your inner self. Just think deep when you want us, and you will find yourself here, or we will come to you; whatever you wish. And if you want to go back, then just close your eyes and see where you want to be," the companion explained. Saif closed his eyes, and when he opened them, he was back on his mat near his book in the deserted place.

Chapter Eight

Saif gathered his belongings and headed back home. With mixed feelings of anxiety, fear, and joy, he rode on the back of his donkey. Anxiety, because he spent three days away from home, traveling through the desert and away from any civilization. He was tired of the little sleep he was getting and because being away from his family made him lonely. Fear, because of not knowing the upcoming; was it good or bad? How will he handle the situation, and most of all, can he keep this secret from everyone? Joy, because he was heading back home. He will meet his mother and his love, Salma, whom he had missed very much. All of these mixed feelings were circulating in his head, which made the trip back home shorter, and just before reaching home, he remembered that he could have used his magic to travel faster and be home in no time, but it was too late now. *"I guess it takes time to get used to using other means,"* he said to himself.

At home, his wife was waiting for him, and as soon as she heard the door open, Salma ran to meet Saif, who was very happy to see her. "So, tell me, how was your trip? Who are the people you visited? Did you have any trouble on the road?" Salma kept asking Saif questions while helping him unload things from the back of his animal. A cat passed by and touched Saif's legs, which made Saif jump. "What is the matter?" asked Salma.

"Nothing," said Saif. The cat made a loud sound and disappeared. Saif smiled, and Salma thought that smile was meant for her and smiled too. "Everything is just fine, my dear. Where is my mother?" Saif asked.

"She went to visit Auntie Aza. She will be back soon," answered Salma. Saif went into the house. Everything sounded the same, except that he would now hear strange sounds from time to time and sometimes see shadows moving very fast.

Salma wants to know all the details of my trip, and I really don't want to lie to her, so what shall I do? He kept thinking. *That cat who came and rubbed herself on me, was she one of them? I don't remember seeing a cat in our house before. Anyway, I need to have some rest, then maybe I can figure out what to tell everybody,* Saif thought.

"Honey, as much as I am glad to see you, I am also very tired, and I need to sleep for a while. Please wake me up for the evening prayer," Saif told his wife. Salma nodded her head and let Saif go to sleep.

Saif lay on the bed and went into a deep sleep. In his sleep, the memory of the last adventure he had with another world came alive. He could see every detail and even could remember all the sounds. The meeting, the gathering, the trees, the landscape, the flying creatures, all presented themselves in front of him like a fantasy story he might have read or been told to him. All seemed so vivid in color and crisp in sound. Something in the dream that kept popping up from time to time, even though he had not seen it in there.

A snake kept watching him from far away every time he glanced at the top left corner of the hall. He could not recollect the reality of that snake, yet while he was recalling the old man speech, the snake started moving slowly towards him. He tried his best to ignore it and concentrate on what was going on around him. When the old man shouted, 'Will you be our leader?' the snake jumped and coiled around Saif's throat. He tried breathing, but felt suffocated. He started shouting for help and felt that his whole body was shaking. "Help, help!" he shouted in his dream, but who will help him here? "Please, somebody, help." He grabbed the snake by its tail and felt a heavy shake in his body.

"Wake up, wake up," was the sound of Salma. "It is time for the evening prayer," she told him. Saif opened his eyes, and he was very thankful that the dream was over. His sweat soaked the bed, and he was shaking like a naked man in a snowy storm. "Are you alright?" Salma asked him.

"Yeah, it was just a bad dream," Saif replied.

Saif went on with his life. People were flocking to his home. Some seeking remedy from certain illness, some trying to find lost items, some wanting to make sure that their wives still love them, and so on. With all of this work, Saif became very busy all day, and he merely had time to go to the field. He decided to hand over the field work to his best friend, Khalfan, and split the income in two equal halves. Khalfan was more than happy to work on Saif's field and made sure to tell Saif about all the activities he conducted in the field. With the aid of his book, Saif became an expert in folk medicine. He used to go to valleys to collect berries and wild plants, which he used for his medicine. The leaves of certain trees were good for headaches after drying, grounding, and sieving them. The roots of another plant were good for asthma and acted as painkillers. The crops of some plants were good for fertility, pregnancy symptoms, and so on. All of these and the aid of his friend from the other world had made a strong ground for him to be famous. People also started calling him "Sheikh El Jin" since he seemed to have an answer for most of their dilemmas. Saif's dilemma was still not sorted out, and the noises and the swift scenes still kept annoying him. He decided to go back again to the other world and sort out most of these hallucinating dreams that he saw whenever he went to sleep.

As soon as he met his companion in the other world, Saif wasted no time to start asking questions. "Tell me, for how long do I have to live with these illusions and restless time?" Saif asked.

"What do you mean?" the companion answered with another question.

"Well, whenever I go to sleep, I see things, hear different voices, and dream bad dreams. One time, I dreamed of snake chocking me, and if it hadn't been for my wife, that nightmare would have killed me," Saif told his companion, who started laughing. "What is so funny?" Saif asked.

"Oh, Ashoor is giving you a hard time!" the companion said and went on explaining. "Remember the first time you were here? Well, you really did not see all of us."

Saif interrupted, "What do you mean?"

The companion replied, "As with your society, there are the good and the bad ones; the same here. We have the good ones whom you have seen as humans and the bad ones who were present but did not reveal themselves, and when they do, they will imitate any creature but not humans. The snake you saw is the devil's leader in our community. His name is Ashoor. He knew that you were coming, and he opposed appointing to you as our head, but he was defeated in the voting of our council. He will try to scare you, but he will never be able to harm you. So next time you have one of these bad dreams, just take a grip of sand and throw it in his direction, and he will leave instantly," the companion explained to Saif. "Now for the images and sounds you are experiencing; it is only a matter of time until you get used to them. You have to remember that in your life, you are sharing two worlds, and that is not easy. It takes courage and patience, which I am sure you have, or else we wouldn't have chosen you. Is everything clear to you now?" the companion asked.

Saif nodded his head, and then he said, "I have seen some of your males in that meeting, but are you a dual gender, I mean, male and female?" he asked.

The companion smiled and said, "See, our community is no different than yours. Historically, when the creator created our ancestors, he asked them to make a wish, and our leader at that time made a plea to his creator that we can see and not be seen and that we can inhabit any part of this world. And so, we were created in such a way that we can emulate any creature and we can live anywhere. Same as humans, we have both genders, and we go through the same process of life and death, but our time is different and our domain is different. In your next visit, I will show you some other species, be it children, youth, old, and even female," the companion explained. Saif departed with his companion, and he was back in his house.

Chapter Nine

People gathered in the town hall to discuss what they were going to do with the dates they had cultivated in the community fields. Some suggested selling it and using the money to improve town services, and some suggested distributing the dates to the poor. Between this opinion and that opinion, Saif arrived at the town hall. All the gathering stood up to greet him, and then they were all seated on the rugs with their backs leaning on a pillow, which separated them from the wall. Khalfan's father spoke to him.

"We are not sure what to do with the dates we cultivated this year from the community field, and we seek your advice." Saif was quiet for some time, staring at the rug below him, then he raised his head and asked the gathering.

"Will you all agree with what I am going to suggest to you?" he asked.

Khalfan's father replied, "We have known you as a man with wisdom and intelligent thinking, and I speak for all that your judgment will be highly appreciated from everyone here."

"We should divide the dates into three equal shares: one share for the poor, one share for the people who worked on it, and the last share to be sold in the market and the money to be used for taking care of the palm trees." All the people agreed with his wise advice and admired his intellectual thinking.

"Saif, Saif," a caller came rushing to him.

"What is the matter, my dear?" Saif inquired.

"Congratulations. Your wife has delivered twins, a boy and a girl," the caller addressed Saif. Saif raised his both hands to the sky and thanked his lord for this blessing. All the gathering started congratulating him on the new comers, and he responded with gratitude and a smile. Khalfan came to him and gave him a big hug.

"Two in one time!" he said jokingly. "So, what are you going to name them?" he asked. Saif smiled cheerfully.

"The boy will be called Ahmed and the girl, Asma," he announced, "and tomorrow, the lunch will be on me for everybody," he said, waving his hand to the gathering.

Saif went home to see his wife and the little children. Salma was lying on the bed, and beside her lay the two toddlers. The midwife who delivered the babies asked him to be quiet since the babies and their mother were sleeping. He walked in on his toes and slowly gave a kiss to his wife and the twins. "May God bless them and bring them to be good children," his mother prayed. Saif took his mother's hand and kissed it. Drops of tears ran down his cheeks. When he raised his head, his semi-white beard was soaking in tears.

"It is the tears of joy, Mama, and I also wish that Grandpa was here today to share this beautiful moment with us," Saif said to his mother. His mother started sobbing with tears, and she hugged Saif very tightly to her body. "Thank you for being a fine man," she said.

Saif continued his life, raising the two kids, whom he adored very much, taking care of his mother and wife, and fulfilling his duties toward everyone that sought his help or required his assistant. The other world now became more familiar, and the strange sounds and shadows did not seem to bother him anymore. Several times, he got called to the other word to sort out different issues. Some of these issues had to do with humans trying to intrude in the other world, and some had to do with performing some religious rituals for their folks in the other world. In all his visits, he still had not encountered a female, and he said to himself, *Maybe my companion has broken his promise. I will bring up the subject with him again next time I see him.*

"I know that I have not fulfilled my promise to you of showing you the opposite sex, but it is just that I was waiting for the right moment. Now the time has come if you want to see the Jin female. You have to remember to think in what form you would like to see them," his companion told him when they met.

"I would rather see them in a form that is very familiar to me, the human form," Saif said.

"Well, you just got your wish," the companion lifted him from one arm and flew with him on the top of a big tree. "See there, below you, can you see nicely?" the companion pointed at a shadow.

"Yes, I can see a shadow only," Saif replied.

"Wait, she is just waking up," the companion told him. Saif looked, and what a beautiful scene he could see! He saw a woman with a beauty that he had never seen in his life. The woman had long black hair that covered her back, a slim waist, rose-red cheeks, and a figure that complimented every part of her body. Saif was speechless for some time. "So, what do you think?" the companion asked.

"I think she is a piece from heaven," Saif replied.

"Do you know whose daughter she is?" Saif asked. "Do you remember the old man you met in your first visit?" asked the companion.

"Yes," answered Saif.

"Well, that is his daughter," said the companion. "Now that you have seen the female, you have got to remember that you have seen her in the human form, but in reality, she can be in any form," the companion told him. "So don't be seduced by the beauty you saw today, because maybe the next time you see her, she might be a scorpion crawling under your bed or a lizard climbing a wall," the companion went on. Saif didn't care much, and all he could think of was that woman.

When Saif returned home that night, the image of the lady he saw never left him. He kept seeing her face wherever he looked. He tried hard to forget her, but without success. *I wonder if she is involved with someone for marriage. If not, can I marry her?* Saif kept wondering. *But how would the marriage be? And will her folks agree? Well, there is only one way to find out,* he said to himself.

After three days, Saif went back to the other world, but this time with a mission. He went to his companion. He expressed his feelings and desire to marry the girl he saw that day. "But you don't even know her name!" the companion exclaimed.

Saif realized that he did not even ask about her name and shyly asked, "Please tell me what her name is."

"That's so typical of you humans; you always rush into things!" the companion said it with irritation. "If you must know, her name is Xelda," the companion said. "What you are asking for is unprecedented. Never before has a human gotten married to a woman from our world; this is just insane!" the companion explained.

"Then I will have to speak to Xelda's father and explain to him my wish," Saif argued.

"You are really serious about this issue?" the companion exclaimed.

"As serious as I can be," Saif insisted.

"Well then, let's go and meet the father," the companion said. They went to see Xelda's father, who was busy educating some of his young children.

"I request permission to speak to you, my lord, in a serious matter." The companion approached the father while Saif waited away.

"Is it very important?" the father asked.

"I am afraid so," the companion replied. The father left the class and came to the companion.

"What seems to be the matter?" he asked.

"I have our sheikh here who wants to approach you in a private matter," the companion said.

"Why keep our sheikh waiting? Tell him to come in," the father told the companion.

"Peace to everyone," Saif greeted the father.

"Peace to you too," the father replied.

"Yes, Sheikh Saif, how can I help you?" the father inquired.

"You see, I have accepted your nomination for me to serve you and your folks as your sheikh, and I have become accustomed to this world. To strengthen that bond between us, I seek your permission to marry your beautiful daughter, Xelda," Saif addressed the father, who was quiet and listening.

"You really surprised me with this request. What you are asking for has never been done before. I will have to take Xelda's agreement first, then the Jin council has to meet and decide on this sensitive matter," the father said. "Give me three days, and I will see what I can do," the father told Saif.

"Well then, we will meet after three days, and I hope that I will hear good news," said Saif.

"I hope so," said the father. "Now, if you will excuse me, I have to finish teaching those kids before they fly away." The father left, leaving the companion and Saif.

Saif waited three days, and it seemed like a century. He was studying all the possibilities and prepared an answer to any obstacle that would hurdle his holy matrimony. After three days, he escorted his companion to Xelda's father's house to hear from him the final verdict of the Jin council on his plea. "It was a tough case, and one of the most difficult cases that we had seen in this council. The folks argued for two nights, and then we came to a vote in which I conveyed to you the result." The father told him when they met. "The good news is that Xelda and I agreed for the marriage, but the Council agreed under the following conditions:

1- Xelda should always appear to you in the form of a human when you are together.
2- Xelda will never be allowed to leave our world.

3- You two should not have any children.

4- And, finally, this marriage should not to be known in the human world.

"Now if you agree to those terms, then you have to sign this marriage contract prepared by the council, having all the above terms." The father handed Saif the marriage document written on a sheet of roses and flowers. Saif read the document very carefully, and then he signed his name with the title of Sheikh El Jin.

"Congratulation! You are now officially married to my daughter. Give us one week to prepare the bride for you," the father told him. Saif thanked the old Jin and left with his companion.

Chapter Ten

In the town hall, a strange man sat there, arguing that magic is not real and that the idea of thinking that there is another world is bogus. Saif sat and listened to the man, whom he was told came from another town and wanted to challenge everyone to prove his point of view. The hall was packed with people, and voices started rising from every corner. Saif held firmly to the stick he had on his right hand, and then suddenly he let go. The stick was transformed into a big snake, which started crawling toward the strange man. Everybody stood up, and they were afraid of the scene of the snake crawling until it stopped in front of the strange man. The man was shaking, and he did not know what to do. He was very confused and afraid. He shouted, "Please, help me and save me from this creature." Everyone looked astonished, and no one knew what to do. Saif took his cap out and threw it toward the snake. The cap transformed into a cat, who took the snake and brought it to Saif. Saif took the snake in his right hand, and it transformed back to a stick. Then he put the cat on his head, and it changed back to a cap. The strange man watched all of this, and started running away, saying, "This is the first and last time I would ever come to this town." Saif smiled cheerfully and asked everyone to be seated. Coffee was presented to everyone, and after finishing, everyone parted to his own affair.

One week had gone, and Saif was ready to get married in the other world. He met his companion, who escorted him to the celebration grounds. All Jin's world was present in this arena. Different shapes of creatures wearing different costumes, jugglers, clowns of all sorts and colors, fire eaters, and men and women dancing on ropes all performing their best acts. Saif sat on the coach near the old man. He watched the celebrations, the music played by frogs and snails, and enjoyed the flying clowns chasing giant monkey. Plenty of food presented everywhere. Saif had not seen such a performance in his life, nor had he seen or ate such delicious meals in his past life. Humming birds then approached, carrying a golden mat, and sat on it in the shape of a woman covered in a dark veil. The birds sang soft songs, and another flock of them sprayed perfume and threw roses at the gathering. Saif stood up as the mat came close by and climbed on it. The birds disappeared, and the mat flown into a big white house. The house was floating in the air and surrounded by a huge garden. The mat stopped at the doorstep, and Saif and his wife stepped out. Saif carried his wife in his arms, and the gate opened. He went into a marvelous hall that led into a bedroom. In the room, Saif took out the veil from his bride, and what an awesome scene he could see. There sat Xelda, smiling and cheerful.

"As customs demand in our world, I have to say my wedding vows, and you have to repeat after me," Xelda told Saif. "We, the creatures from two different worlds, have agreed to love and cherish each other for as long as we live and as agreed in our marriage contract," Xelda cited, and

Saif repeated after her. Saif then took his bride to bed and indulged himself in a world that could never be experienced by any other human being.

Saif went on with his life, raising the kids, and serving the people of both worlds. Salma had been his aid in all these years. She was the throne that held him when he needed affection, the heart that loved him when he needed sympathy, and the mind that guided him when he strayed. To Saif, both Salma and Xelda had their own unique qualities in the world they inhabited. Salma was Saif's first love in the human world. He cherished and loved her. Xelda was his eyes, mind, and heart in the other world, where Saif needed a person that he could trust. Neither Salma nor Xelda knew each other, and they never knew that they shared the same lover. Saif was careful never to let any of them suspect his faithfulness to either of them, but when Salma became sick, Saif could not hide his agony and sadness from Xelda.

"The mother of my children is sick, and I tried everything in the book to cure her, but the illness keeps persisting," Saif told Xelda. "I am afraid that I might lose her," he went on. Xelda listened very carefully, not knowing what to say. As per Saif's description to her of the illness, it seemed very serious, and she knew there was no cure for cancer.

"I only wish there was some way I could help you," Xelda said to Saif while dipping her fingers in his hair and smoothing his cheeks as he lay, putting his head in her lap. "My prayers are with her and you, and may the creator have mercy on her soul," she told him. "Does your mother or the children know that Salma has cancer?" Xelda asked Saif.

"They know that she is sick, but they all have high hopes that I can cure her. They don't know the seriousness of the illness, and I am not going to tell them," Saif said with a sad voice. Saif slept on Xelda's lap, and she patiently took his head and supported him with a pillow.

At home, Saif went to check on Salma. He thought she was sleeping, but when he checked her heart, she was breathless. Saif kissed her on the forehead with drops of tears falling from his eyes like pouring rain. He did not weep; merely sorrow come out in the form of tears. He closed her eyes and then called his mother, who came rushing. She found Saif sitting on the bed beside Salma, and she asked him, "What is the matter, my son?"

"Salma is gone, Mama. Salma is gone," he told her.

After Salma passed away, Saif became lonely in the human world, and he used to spend most of his time in the other world. "The children are still growing, and beside yourself, they need someone to take care of them. You know that I am getting old and my health is not that good, so why don't you find another wife?" his mother told him.

"Now that I am in the mid-fifties, who will agree to marry me?" Saif responded to his mother's demand.

"Leave that to me; I know just the person," his mother told him.

"Any woman I marry, I want her to treat my children like her own, or else I will not marry," Saif said.

"The lady I know is divorced, and she does not have children. Maybe you know her, Sheikha, the tailor's daughter," Saif's mother told him. Saif nodded his head and went out to see his friend, Khalfan.

Saif sat with Khalfan under the tree where their hut used to be. "Remember this place; we had such a good memory in the hut we built. Too bad it is not here anymore," Saif said, leaning his back on the tree trunk.

"Nothing stays the same, look at us how we have grown and how time has changed us," Khalfan answered his friend.

"Ever since Salma died, I have had that empty feeling. What tortures me more is the look on the children's faces and seeing how they miss their mother. Now my mother wants me to marry again. I understand her point of view, which is helpful in raising the kids, but frankly, I am not that enthusiastic about the idea. I have this inner feeling that whomever I marry will not accept the children as her own children," Saif told Khalfan.

"Being a man, you also have your needs to be fulfilled, and maybe the children can see that no one will take over their mother's place, but a soul mate for their father will ease his loneliness," Khalfan consoled his friend.

"Yeah, but you got to remember that the kids are in their early teens only. This is the age when they need a friend more than just a mother, especially Asma," said Saif.

"Why do you assume the worst? Maybe the lady you want to marry will turn out to be nice. By the way, you did not tell me whom you want to marry?" Khalfan poked his friend with his elbow.

"My mother wants me to marry Sheikha, the tailor's daughter. Do you know her?" Saif asked.

"No, but I have heard from my mother that she was married in another town, and she got divorced. I know she has no children, that's all I know about her," Khalfan said it while standing up and pulling Saif to stand up. "It's time for evening prayer, let's go, old man." Khalfan led the way.

Saif got married to Sheikha, and she moved to live with him, his mother, and the children. At first, Sheikha was very friendly with the two children, but after some time, she became jealous and felt that Saif loved his children more than he loved her. That's when all the trouble began. Sheikha would be very happy all day when Saif was outside the house, and as soon as he stepped a foot in the house, she would start complaining about everything. "The place is always a mess because of your kids. They throw everything, and they never help with the house chores. They are always noisy, and they don't speak to me with respect," she used to complain. Saif summoned his children and asked them to help with the housework and always respect Sheikha. What Saif didn't know that Sheikha was lying and that she did not do anything accept sleeping, eating, and taking care of her body. She used to treat the children like slaves and used to shout at Asma for everything she did. Saif's mother knew everything, and she was hoping that Saif would find out the truth himself, but when she saw that things were getting out of hand, she requested Saif to divorce his wife.

"But, Mother, you are the one who recommended her!" Saif said.

"If I had known her like this, I wouldn't have even advised you to marry her, but I made a mistake," Saif's mother told him.

"OK, Mother, I have another idea. I will split the house into two sections. One will be for me and Sheikha, and one for you and the kids. This way, I will see if she is going to complain again," Saif said. Saif's mother agreed to her son's proposal.

As the saying goes, that the shadow can never be straight if the stem is twisted, so was Sheikha's behavior; it never gets better. She continued whining and complaining. Then, finally, after five years, Saif decided that he had it. He told Sheikha that she was divorced and she could go to her family. Saif took that partition that separated the house in two and reunited with his mother and children. During all these five years which Saif put up with Sheikha, he used to find his vanity with Xelda. He would spend longer time with her, and sometimes he would spend the whole day with her.

The children were now in adulthood. Asma was engaged to a man from another town, whereas Ahmed married Khalfan's daughter. Asma left the house to live with her husband, and Ahmed stayed with his father and grandmother. His grandmother got sick. She was old now and suffered from diabetes and high blood pressure. Saif tried to take care of his mother, but without avail. She passed away a year after Saif divorced Sheikha.

Saif was also getting old, and his heath was not as it used to be. He tried reducing his activities and spending more quality time with his grandchildren from Ahmed and Asma.

Time flew by, and one day, while Saif was praying, he collapsed. Ahmed tried reviving him, but death was faster than Ahmed's will. Saif's death was announced in both worlds, and both worlds mourned him. He was laid to rest in the nearby cemetery beside his mother and his grandfather's grave. And the other world made a symbolic funeral for him, and they went along with humans for his burial without being detected or noticed. "Sheikh El Jin is gone, is gone, is gone," they chanted, coming back from the cemetery.

www.ingramcontent.com/pod-product-compliance
Lightning Source LLC
Chambersburg PA
CBHW051130160726
47997CB00018B/1106